for WILLIE

SEASONS

SEASONS

by John Burningham

Jonathan Cape London

First published 1969
Reprinted 1970, 1972, 1974, 1976, 1979, 1981, 1987, 1993
© 1969 by John Burningham
Jonathan Cape Ltd, 20 Vauxhall Bridge Road, London SW1V 2SA
ISBN 0 224 61628 5
Printed in Hong Kong
Typography and title-page design by Jan Pieńkowski

Spring is

birds nesting

pigs rooting

lambs playing

ducks dabbling

and flowers

Summer is

ripening corn

holidays

buzzing insects

heat waves

and thunder storms

Autumn is

leaves flying

squirrels hoarding
tractors ploughing

bonfires,
and geese soaring

longer nights

Winter is

foggy days

frost at night

ice and snow

and endless rain

then it's Spring